THE TALE
OF
TWO BAD MICE

THE TALE OF
TWO BAD MICE

By
BEATRIX POTTER

Author of
" The Tale of Peter Rabbit " &c.

BLOOMSBURY BOOKS
in association with
FREDERICK WARNE

BLOOMSBURY BOOKS IN ASSOCIATION WITH FREDERICK WARNE

Published by the Penguin Group
Penguin Books Ltd, 27 Wrights Lane, London W8 5TZ, England
Penguin Books USA Inc., 375 Hudson Street, New York, N.Y. 10014, USA
Penguin Books Australia Ltd, Ringwood, Victoria, Australia
Penguin Books Canada Ltd, 10 Alcorn Avenue, Toronto, Ontario, Canada M4V 3B2
Penguin Books (N.Z.) Ltd, 182-190 Wairau Road, Auckland 10, New Zealand

Penguin Books Ltd, Registered Offices: Harmondsworth, Middlesex, England

Bloomsbury Books, an imprint of The Godfrey Cave Group,
42 Bloomsbury Street, London WC1B 3QJ

First published by Frederick Warne & Co. 1904
Published with new reproductions 1987
This edition first published 1993

ISBN 1 85471 350 7

Printed and bound in Great Britain by
William Clowes Limited, Beccles and London

FOR

W. M. L. W.

THE LITTLE GIRL
WHO HAD THE DOLL'S HOUSE

ONCE upon a time there was a very beautiful doll's-house; it was red brick with white windows, and it had real muslin curtains and a front door and a chimney.

IT belonged to two Dolls called Lucinda and Jane, at least it belonged to Lucinda, but she never ordered meals.

Jane was the Cook; but she never did any cooking, because the dinner had been bought ready-made, in a box full of shavings.

12

THERE were two red lobsters and a ham, a fish, a pudding, and some pears and oranges.

They would not come off the plates, but they were extremely beautiful.

ONE morning Lucinda and Jane had gone out for a drive in the doll's perambulator. There was no one in the nursery, and it was very quiet. Presently there was a little scuffling, scratching noise in a corner near the fireplace, where there was a hole under the skirting-board.

Tom Thumb put out his head for a moment, and then popped it in again.

Tom Thumb was a mouse.

A MINUTE afterwards, Hunca Munca, his wife, put her head out, too; and when she saw that there was no one in the nursery, she ventured out on the oilcloth under the coalbox.

THE doll's-house stood at the other side of the fire-place. Tom Thumb and Hunca Munca went cautiously across the hearthrug. They pushed the front door—it was not fast.

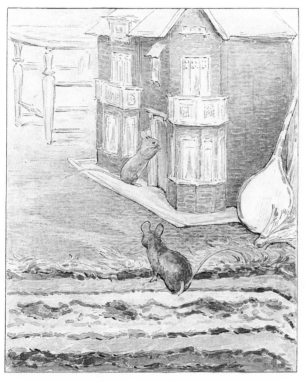

TOM THUMB and
Hunca Munca went
upstairs and peeped into the
dining-room. Then they
squeaked with joy!

Such a lovely dinner was
laid out upon the table! There
were tin spoons, and lead
knives and forks, and two
dolly-chairs—all *so* convenient!

TOM THUMB set to work at once to carve the ham. It was a beautiful shiny yellow, streaked with red.

The knife crumpled up and hurt him; he put his finger in his mouth.

"It is not boiled enough; it is hard. You have a try, Hunca Munca."

24

HUNCA MUNCA stood up in her chair, and chopped at the ham with another lead knife.

"It's as hard as the hams at the cheesemonger's," said Hunca Munca.

THE ham broke off the plate with a jerk, and rolled under the table.

"Let it alone," said Tom Thumb; "give me some fish, Hunca Munca!"

28

HUNCA MUNCA tried every tin spoon in turn; the fish was glued to the dish.

Then Tom Thumb lost his temper. He put the ham in the middle of the floor, and hit it with the tongs and with the shovel—bang, bang, smash, smash!

The ham flew all into pieces, for underneath the shiny paint it was made of nothing but plaster!

THEN there was no end to
the rage and disappoint-
ment of Tom Thumb and
Hunca Munca. They broke
up the pudding, the lobsters,
the pears and the oranges.

As the fish would not come
off the plate, they put it into
the red-hot crinkly paper fire
in the kitchen; but it would
not burn either.

32

TOM THUMB went up the kitchen chimney and looked out at the top—there was no soot.

WHILE Tom Thumb was up the chimney, Hunca Munca had another disappointment. She found some tiny canisters upon the dresser, labelled—Rice—Coffee—Sago—but when she turned them upside down, there was nothing inside except red and blue beads.

THEN those mice set to work to do all the mischief they could—especially Tom Thumb! He took Jane's clothes out of the chest of drawers in her bedroom, and he threw them out of the top floor window.

But Hunca Munca had a frugal mind. After pulling half the feathers out of Lucinda's bolster, she remembered that she herself was in want of a feather bed.

WITH Tom Thumb's assist-
ance she carried the
bolster downstairs, and across
the hearthrug. It was diffi-
cult to squeeze the bolster into
the mouse-hole; but they
managed it somehow.

39

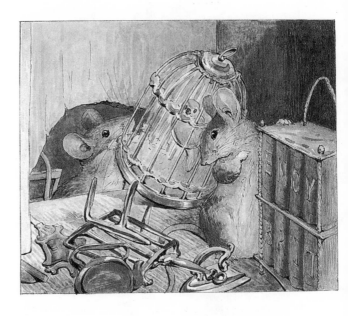

40

THEN Hunca Munca went back and fetched a chair, a book-case, a bird-cage, and several small odds and ends. The book-case and the bird-cage refused to go into the mouse-hole.

HUNCA MUNCA left them behind the coalbox, and went to fetch a cradle.

HUNCA MUNCA was just returning with another chair, when suddenly there was a noise of talking outside upon the landing. The mice rushed back to their hole, and the dolls came into the nursery.

WHAT a sight met the eyes
of Jane and Lucinda!
Lucinda sat upon the upset
kitchen stove and stared; and
Jane leant against the kitchen
dresser and smiled—but nei-
ther of them made any remark.

47

THE book-case and the bird-cage were rescued from under the coal-box—but Hunca Munca has got the cradle, and some of Lucinda's clothes.

SHE also has some useful pots and pans, and several other things.

52

THE little girl that the doll's-house belonged to, said,—"I will get a doll dressed like a policeman!"

B^{UT} the nurse said,—"I will set a mouse-trap!"

54

SO that is the story of the two Bad Mice,—but they were not so very very naughty after all, because Tom Thumb paid for everything he broke.

He found a crooked sixpence under the hearthrug; and upon Christmas Eve, he and Hunca Munca stuffed it into one of the stockings of Lucinda and Jane.

AND very early every morning—before anybody is
awake—Hunca Munca comes
with her dust-pan and her
broom to sweep the Dollies'
house!

THE END